# LITTLE MISS TROUBLE
## Changes Colour

Roger Hargreaves

MR. MEN    LITTLE MISS

MR. MEN™ LITTLE MISS™ © THOIP (a SANRIO company)

Little Miss Trouble Changes Colour © 2014 THOIP (a SANRIO company)
Printed and published under licence from Price Stern Sloan, Inc., Los Angeles.
First published in France 1997 by Hachette Livre
This edition published in 2015 by Dean, an imprint of Egmont UK Limited,
The Yellow Building, 1 Nicholas Road, London W11 4AN

ISBN 978 0 6035 7004 9
58244/2
Printed in Great Britain

EGMONT

Little Miss Trouble wasn't called Trouble for nothing. She may look very sweet but, believe me, she means trouble!

On this particular morning, Little Miss Trouble was making a phone call. A troublesome phone call! She was pretending to be Little Miss Shy and she had invited Mr Noisy round for tea.

Hee! Hee! Hee!

Who's that laughing?

Little Miss Trouble!

But that was just one of her many troublesome tricks. Look what she did to Mr Small!

She covered his house with a large box.

When Mr Small woke up the next morning, he found his house was completely dark so he just rolled over and went back to sleep.

Hee! Hee! Hee!

Who's that laughing?

Little Miss Trouble!

And that's not all. She also went to the furniture shop.

"Good morning," she said cheerfully to the lady in the shop. "Mr Mean has sent me to buy some beautiful armchairs from your shop. Please send him the bill."

Hee! Hee! Hee!

Who's that laughing?

Little Miss Trouble, again!

Poor Mr Mean!

When the armchairs were delivered to his house he thought he might faint.

And when he saw the bill he really did faint!

Hee! Hee! Hee!

Who's that laughing?

Little Miss Trouble, of course!

Enough was enough. Little Miss Trouble needed to be taught a lesson.

"Oh, I'm so very, very clever," announced Mr Clever to his friends. "I have the cleverest idea to get our own back on Little Miss Trouble."

Would you like to know what his plan was? Of course you would. Well it's quite simple. Just take a look at Mr Clever's drawing.

Hee! Hee! Hee!

Who's that laughing now?

It's Little Miss Trouble's friends!

The next morning, as always, Little Miss Trouble had lots of good ideas for causing trouble.

She met Little Miss Sunshine in the street.

"What has happened to you, Little Miss Trouble?" exclaimed Little Miss Sunshine. "You're blue! Completely blue!"

"Really?" said Little Miss Trouble, very surprised.

"If I were you, I'd see a doctor," said Little Miss Sunshine.

Hee! Hee! Hee!

Who's that laughing?

It's not Little Miss Trouble!

Little Miss Trouble went into the greengrocer's shop.

"Why is she blue?" said a very confused Mr Dizzy. "Has she been drinking ink?"

"What if we all catch it?" worried Mr Fussy. "You should stay in bed if you're ill."

"Does it itch?" asked Little Miss Magic.

Hee! Hee! Hee!

Little Miss Trouble started to worry.

Outside the shop she met Mr Funny.

"What a beautiful blue colour you are Little Miss Trouble," he said. "That colour really does suit you wonderfully."

"I don't know what you're talking about," replied Little Miss Trouble, crossly.

"Well the strange illness you have, of course," said Mr Funny, suddenly serious.

Hee! Hee! Hee!

Who's that laughing?

It's not Little Miss Trouble!

And by now Little Miss Trouble was feeling really quite troubled.

Little Miss Trouble had to find out what was going on. As quickly as she could, she ran to the town paint shop.

"Tell me, Mr Paintbrush," she said hurriedly. "What colour would you say I was?"

"Hmm, let me see," he replied. "Let me look at you closely."

"Well?" said Little Miss Trouble, impatiently, after several minutes had passed.

"Blue," said Mr Paintbrush. "Definitely blue. Decidedly blue. Sky blue!"

"But this is terrible," said Little Miss Trouble. "Is there anything you can do to help me?"

"I have exactly what you need," replied Mr Paintbrush. "Tip this into your bath and you'll soon be back to normal." And he handed her a small packet.

The next morning Little Miss Trouble was looking very pleased with herself.

"Good morning, Little Miss Trouble," said Mr Silly. "What a pretty colour! As blue as the bluest sky!"

"Such a wonderful colour," agreed Little Miss Sunshine.

"Fabulous," nodded Mr Small. "But I do hope you spoke to a doctor?"

"Are you sure you feel quite well?" said Little Miss Magic.

Hee! Hee! Hee!

Everyone started laughing.

Everyone except Little Miss Trouble, that is.

She didn't understand what was going on.

But at that moment it began to rain.

And as the rain fell on Little Miss Trouble, little by little the blue started to wash away until soon there was nothing more than a big blue puddle at her feet.

Hee! Hee! Hee!

Who's that laughing?

It's Little Miss Trouble and her friends!

"That was a very good trick," laughed Little Miss Trouble.

She had got her old colour back again, and her smile, but, unluckily for her friends …

… her troublesome ways were back, too!

They'd better look out!